Li'l Bratz™
Lights, Camera, Star!

GROSSET & DUNLAP
Published by the Penguin Group
Penguin Group (USA) Inc., 375 Hudson Street, New York, New York 10014, U.S.A.
Penguin Group (Canada), 10 Alcorn Avenue, Toronto, Ontario, Canada M4V 3B2
(a division of Pearson Penguin Canada Inc.)
Penguin Books Ltd, 80 Strand, London WC2R 0RL, England
Penguin Ireland, 25 St Stephen's Green, Dublin 2, Ireland
(a division of Penguin Books Ltd)
Penguin Group (Australia), 250 Camberwell Road, Camberwell, Victoria 3124, Australia
(a division of Pearson Australia Group Pty Ltd)
Penguin Books India Pvt Ltd, 11 Community Centre, Panchsheel Park, New Delhi - 110 017, India
Penguin Group (NZ), Cnr Airborne and Rosedale Roads, Albany, Auckland 1310, New Zealand
(a division of Pearson New Zealand Ltd)
Penguin Books (South Africa) (Pty) Ltd, 24 Sturdee Avenue, Rosebank, Johannesburg 2196, South Africa

Penguin Books Ltd, Registered Offices: 80 Strand, London WC2R 0RL, England

www.bratzpack.com
TM & © MGA Entertainment, Inc. Lil' Bratz and all related logos, names and distinctive likenesses are the exclusive property of MGA Entertainment, Inc. All Rights Reserved.

Used under license by Penguin Young Readers Group. Published in 2005 by Grosset & Dunlap, a division of Penguin Young Readers Group, 345 Hudson Street, New York, New York 10014. GROSSET & DUNLAP is a trademark of Penguin Group (USA) Inc. Printed in the U.S.A.

ISBN 0-448-43921-2   10 9 8 7 6 5 4 3 2 1

Lil' Bratz™

Lights, Camera, Star!

Grosset & Dunlap

Talia spotted Nazalia in the lunchroom with her head buried in her sketchbook. Lunch was their favorite time of day because they got to hang with their best buds!

"Hey, Naz," said Talia, sitting down next to her friend. "What are you drawing?"

"I'm designing some hip outfits for Ailani and me for our dance number in the talent show!" Nazalia said. "Check 'em out!"

"Wow! Those look awesome!" answered Talia.

Just then Ailani and Zada walked in. "Hey, girls—great news!" said Zada. "I just found out that I get to be the MC for the school talent show! Just call me MC Zada."

The girls were excited for her, but Talia looked a little down in the dumps. "I have no idea what I could do for the talent show," she said.

Ailani jumped in. "Don't worry, Talia. We'll figure out something. You're great at lots of things! We'll get you in the spotlight for sure!"

Later that night the girls were hangin' out in Zada's bedroom, thinking of talent ideas for Talia.

"Why don't you dance with me and Naz?" Ailani suggested. "We'd make a smashing trio!"

But Talia was too nervous to dance in front of everybody.

"How 'bout you perform a speech from a play? I could help you rehearse," offered Nazalia.

"That's not really my thing," said Talia.

"Hey, I've got an idea," said Zada. "Can you play an instrument?"

But Talia shook her head sadly.

Just then the girls' fave song came on the radio blastin' from Zada's boom box. It was just what the girls needed to cheer them up! The girls danced around the room to the music.

Suddenly, Talia jumped up onto the bed, took hold of a hair-brush, and used it as a microphone. She started belting out the words to the song. Could she sing? Totally!

It was finally time for the show.

Zada was a fantastic MC.

Ailani and Nazalia
wowed the crowd with
their funky hip-hop sound
and jivin' dance moves.

Talia shone as a true star when she sang her
tunes. Everyone showed off their special talents!

At the end of the show, Zada came back to the front of the stage. "Everyone was simply amazing! We have tons of talented students here—and everyone is going to get a special ribbon for participating! But now it's time to choose your favorite performer. The winner will be decided by whoever gets the loudest applause. Are you ready to start your clappin' and cheerin'?"

As each name was called, the applause got louder and louder. Talia was nervous for her name to be called. *What if no one claps?* she thought. She shut her eyes tightly as Zada shouted, "And give it up for Talia!"

Everyone yelled and cheered. "Talia! Talia! Talia!"

"And the winner is . . ." Zada announced proudly, "Talia—by a landslide!"

Talia couldn't believe she had won! Zada presented her with
the prize. She thanked her friends as she accepted the trophy.
"I never would've been able to sing in front of everyone
without my fave girls cheerin' me on! Come up here, girls—you
have to share the spotlight with me!"

With her friends at her side, Talia declared,
"You're the best friends a girl could have!"